Archie and
Frisbee

For Freddie and Frisbee, George and Squiggle

First published in 2013
by Wayland

Text copyright © Anne Rooney
Illustration copyright © Ann Johns

Wayland
338 Euston Road
London NW1 3BH

Wayland Australia
Level 17/207 Kent Street
Sydney, NSW 2000

Series Editor: Louise John
Cover design: D.R.ink
Design: Lisa Peacock
Consultant: Shirley Bickler

A CIP catalogue record for this book is available from the British Library.

ISBN 9780750268707

Printed in China

Wayland is a division of Hachette Children's Books,
an Hachette UK Company

www.hachette.co.uk

Archie and Frisbee

Written by Anne Rooney
Illustrated by Ann Johns

WAYLAND

Camilla was taking Frisbee home for the weekend.

"You can take him next weekend, Archie," Miss Nitwit said. "If you're good."

Archie hated being good.
But he really wanted to take
Frisbee home. On Monday he
sharpened all the pencils.

On Tuesday he cleaned the
fish tank.

On Wednesday he put the books away.

On Thursday he put the art things away.

"I've been good all week,"
Archie said. "Please can I take
Frisbee home?"

"You've been very helpful,"
Miss Nitwit said. "Yes, you
can take Frisbee home."

"Be careful," Camilla said.
"Don't let him run away."
"Of course I won't!" said Archie.

Frisbee's cage went on the back seat of Dad's car. "Don't let him escape," Dad said.

The car got stuck in traffic.
Archie opened the cage and
Frisbee ran up Archie's sleeve.

When the car stopped, Archie put Frisbee in his school bag.

"Put that cage in your room, Archie," Mum said. "Make sure Frisbee doesn't get out."

Archie put the cage and his bag in his room.

On Saturday, Archie played with Frisbee all day.

He gave some of his lunch to Frisbee. He let him run around his room.

At bedtime, Archie couldn't find
Frisbee. He looked everywhere.

"I'll be in so much trouble!"
Archie said.

"You should have been more
careful," Lucy said.

"What can I do?" Archie cried.
"You should have been more
careful," Dad said.

"I'm so unhappy!" Archie cried. "I love Frisbee! Where can he be?"

"You should have been more careful," Mum said. "Now, get in the car, Archie."

Mum drove Archie to the pet shop. "Find one that looks just like Frisbee," Mum said.

They put the new hamster in Frisbee's cage. "You have to tell Miss Nitwit," Mum said.

Archie took the new hamster
to school on Monday.
It looked just like Frisbee.
No one could tell.

Archie didn't tell Miss Nitwit
he'd lost Frisbee.

"Aaaah!" Camilla screamed.
"There's something coming
out of Archie's bag!"

Something small and furry
ran across the floor.
It was Frisbee!

"How did Frisbee get out?"
Miss Nitwit asked. She took
Frisbee back to his cage.

But Frisbee was already in the cage.

"Frisbee has had a baby!"
shouted Amal.

"No, Amal," Miss Nitwit said. "Frisbee has not had a baby. Frisbee is a boy."

"What is going on, Archie?"
asked Miss Nitwit, crossly.

"I lost Frisbee," he said, at last.
"We bought another hamster."

"You should have been more careful," Miss Nitwit said.

"Can we keep them both?" asked Camilla. "Frisbee can have a new friend."

"Yes," Miss Nitwit laughed. "But it is Archie's job to clean out the cage!"

START READING is a series of highly enjoyable books for beginner readers. The books have been carefully graded to match the Book Bands widely used in schools. This enables readers to be sure they choose books that match their own reading ability.

Look out for the Band colour on the book in our Start Reading logo.

The Bands are:

Pink Band 1

Red Band 2

Yellow Band 3

Blue Band 4

Green Band 5

Orange Band 6

Turquoise Band 7

Purple Band 8

Gold Band 9

START READING books can be read independently or shared with an adult. They promote the enjoyment of reading through satisfying stories supported by fun illustrations.

Anne Rooney has written lots of books for children including the All About Henry stories for this series. Have a look! She lives in a state of chaos with her two daughters, a tortoise called Tor2 and a blue lobster called Marcel.

Ann Johns likes to draw life – busy, lovely life. Birds flying, dogs jumping, people dancing... So always have a pencil handy, because you never know what exciting thing is waiting around the corner for you to draw!